Zoey
AND
SASSAFRAS

MONSTERS AND MOLD

THE INNOVATION PRESS

READ THE REST OF THE SERIES

for activities and more visit

ZOEYANDSASSAFRAS.COM

TABLE OF CONTENTS

FOR CHLOÉ AND JULIEN — ML
FOR GOOSE AND BUBS — AC

Publisher's Cataloging-in-Publication
Citro, Asia, author.
Monsters and mold / Asia Citro ; illustrator, Marion Lindsay.
pages cm -- (Zoey and Sassafras ; 2)
Summary: A girl, Zoey, and her cat, Sassafras use science experiments to help a monster with a problem.
Audience: Grades K-5.
LCCN 2016904045
ISBN 978-1-943147-14-4; ISBN 978-1-943147-13-7; ISBN 978-1-943147-15-1;
ISBN 978-1-943147-16-8; ISBN 978-1-943147-17-5
1. Monsters--Juvenile fiction. 2. Molds (Fungi)--Juvenile fiction. [1. Monsters--Fiction. 2. Molds (Fungi)--Fiction. 3. Science--Experiments--Fiction. 4. Experiments--Fiction.] I. Lindsay, Marion, illustrator. II. Title. III. Series: Citro, Asia. Zoey and Sassafras ; 2.
PZ7.1.C577Mo 2016
[E]
QBI16-600079

Text copyright 2017 by Asia Citro
Illustrations copyright 2017 by Marion Lindsay
Journal entries handwritten by S. Citro

Published by The Innovation Press
P.O. Box 2584, Woodinville, WA 98072-2584
www.theinnovationpress.com

Printed and bound by Worzalla
Production Date: February 2017 | Plant Location: Stevens Point, Wisconsin

Cover design by Nicole LaRue | Book layout by Kerry Ellis

PROLOGUE

These days my cat Sassafras and I are always desperately hoping we'll hear our barn doorbell.

I know most people are excited to hear their doorbell ring. It might mean a present or package delivery, or a friend showing up to play. But our doorbell is even more exciting than that. Because it's a *magic* doorbell. When it rings, it means there's a magical animal waiting outside our barn. A magical animal who needs our help.

My mom's been helping them basically her whole life. And now *I* get to help, too . . .

CHAPTER 1
THE BREAD EXPERIMENTS

Spluuuurk.

I laughed. The sound of the moldy bread squishing inside the ziplock bag was super gross.

So I poked the bag again.

Spluuuurk.

My cat jumped up on the table to see what I was doing. A cool breeze from the window ruffled his fluffy fur, and he squinted in the sunlight. *Spluuuurk.* He jumped backward and hissed.

"It's OK, Sassafras," I said, giggling
and tickling his chin. "The mold is sealed
inside the bag. It won't get you, kitty!"

My cat didn't look convinced.

"It's actually really cool. I'm running

two experiments with the old bread Mom found. See," I said and pointed across the room. "That experiment over there is testing whether wet bread molds faster than dry bread." I poked the bag on the table again. "And this one is testing whether warm bread molds faster than cold bread. That's why it's here in the sun."

Sassafras poked a toe at the bag and wrinkled his nose.

"There are other bags in the fridge and freezer, but they don't have any mold yet. Which means this one is much more fun to look at. Don't you think, kitty?"

Sassafras scrunched up his face and jumped off the table. I guess he didn't enjoy these mold experiments as much as I did.

Maybe he was too busy hoping the magic doorbell would ring. But ever since the sweet baby dragon I'd nursed back to health had left, the doorbell had been disappointingly silent. I was trying to fill my time with experiments to keep my mind busy. Working on science was way more fun than sitting outside my mom's office, waiting and waiting and *waiting* for the sound of the magic doorbell.

I sighed.

Outside the window, there was a rustling in the bushes. Sassafras leapt onto the table. He pointed his ears toward our backyard and held very still, listening.

"You heard that, right?" I whispered to Sassafras.

He meowed once in reply without taking his eyes off the yard. We both pressed our faces to the window screen. Maybe it was a deer? Or a cute little chipmunk?

The bushes rustled again. Then something . . . or *someone* . . . cleared its throat. Sassafras and I jumped!

CHAPTER 2
PARDON ME

My heart pounded and my stomach did flip-flops. I couldn't think of any forest animal that cleared its throat. My mom was out running errands. Should I get my dad? Maybe I'd just imagined that noise... I could think of one way to find out.

"Um, hello? Is someone out there?" I squeaked.

The shrubs parted, and a creature about the same size as me walked out. He was furry, orange, and had giant ears with two horns on top of his head. He squinted at me and Sassafras with his two big eyes. He looked like . . . like . . . a *monster*?

I stood there, frozen, with my mouth hanging open.

The monster brushed his fur off and cleared his throat again. He seemed like he was about to say something. Could monsters *talk*?

Sassafras broke the silence by launching out of my arms. Before I could stop him, he flew out the cat door and raced toward the monster outside. I began to follow, but stopped. That was an awfully tall monster. But then again, I didn't want Sassafras to get hurt. What should I do?

I took a deep breath. Mom never said there were dangerous

magical creatures in our forest. So maybe the monster was really big *and* really friendly? I crossed my fingers that this would be true as I ran outside.

The monster stood with his arms in the air, looking terrified. Sassafras galloped toward him. Once he was close enough, my cat leapt into the air and aimed straight at the monster's chest.

The monster screamed, "What is that? *Eeek!* Help me!" He stumbled backward.

Was my cat trying to leap into the monster's arms? The monster wouldn't keep still, so Sassafras gave up and started *purring* furiously at the

trembling monster's feet. He bumped his head against the monster's legs and kept purring.

The monster put his hands up to his cheeks in horror and shrieked again. "It's trying to eat me! I can hear its tummy growling from here. Oh, help me!"

I scooped Sassafras into my arms. "I'm so sorry! My cat isn't trying to hurt you. I think he just *really* likes you."

Sassafras strained in my arms, wanting to love on the monster more. I squeezed him to my chest a little tighter.

"Likes me enough to eat me!" the monster huffed.

I giggled. "Sassafras eats cat food, not monsters. I promise."

The monster calmed down a bit. He took a closer look at me and wrinkled his face. "I thought you were a bigger human, from the stories I've heard in the forest."

I stood up a bit straighter. "The stories were probably about my mom, but I'm big enough to help you."

The monster raised an eyebrow. "Are you sure? You seem rather small."

I moved Sassafras over to my hip. "I know all about the magic doorbell and the barn. I even helped a baby dragon all by myself."

"Really?" The monster seemed a little more convinced. "I love dragons."

"Me too," I said with a sigh,

remembering little Marshmallow. "I figured out what was wrong with a baby dragon who didn't even speak, so I'm sure I can help you," I added confidently. I mean, really. How hard could this be with someone who could answer questions!

The monster looked me over once more, then he nodded. "As I'm sure you know, it's almost time for the annual Monster Ball."

The Monster Ball? An annual *monster dance*? The thought of a bunch of monsters dancing together almost made me laugh out loud. I didn't want to seem rude, though. I also didn't want to look like I'd never heard of the Monster Ball. So I nodded and smiled.

"Well, anyway, it's coming up in a few days," he continued. "For as long as I can remember, I've, uh, had a bit of an embarrassing problem. And because of it, I've never gone to the big dance. But I'd really like to go this year. I was hoping you could help me get rid of it."

At this, he turned around. I gasped. The monster's fur was covered in mold!

CHAPTER 3
MOLDY FUR

The monster turned back, but kept his eyes on the ground. "It's disgusting. I know."

"Oh! Sorry! It's not that bad, really," I said. "I was surprised, that's all. I've never seen mold on fur before. But then again, I've never seen monster fur. Is this something that happens to lots of monsters?"

"No, just to me." He sighed sadly. "It's *so* embarrassing. We monsters take great care with our appearance. But no matter how often I bathe, this awful mold always grows. It starts on my back and spreads until I'm covered with it!"

"I'm so sorry." I felt bad for the poor monster. What a terrible problem to have.

"Can you help me? There must be some way to stop the mold from growing in my fur."

"I'd be happy to help. Ummm, I could . . ." I pressed a finger to my lips in thought. Molds can be dangerous. I'd need to think of a solution where I didn't touch the mold, or I'd have to wait until my mom was home to help.

Sassafras meowed. Then he reached a paw up and bopped me on the head!

"Hey! What was that for?" I frowned at him. But then I realized Sassafras was reminding me to use my Thinking Goggles. It sounds silly, but it always works. Wearing my lucky pair of goggles on my head always gives me fantastic ideas.

"Um, just a minute, Mr. Monster. I'll be right back. I've got to grab something from our house."

The monster humphed. "My name is Gorp. Not Mr. Monster."

"Oh, sorry, Gorp! One second."

As soon as I put my Thinking Goggles on, I thought of more questions to ask. Phew. I could probably figure out this whole problem before my mom got home. I grabbed a pen and my science journal and ran outside.

I adjusted my Thinking Goggles and opened my science journal. It flipped to the page with the photo of Sassafras riding Marshmallow the dragon. I slowly ran my fingers over the photo. The shimmering light from Marshmallow's scales jumped right out of the page. It made the magical photo seem alive.

Gorp cleared his throat.

I quickly found a new page in my journal and wrote my problem at the top:

PROBLEM:

Gorp's fur is molding.

"So Gorp, how often do you take a bath? And where?"

"I bathe every day in the stream."

"And then what? You dry off and go home to your . . . monster house?"

"Well, sort of. I shake my fur off, and then I go sleep in my warm cave up in the mountains."

I wrote down:

NOTES:

Bath in stream.

(Damp) fur.

sleeps in (warm) cave.

Aha! That was it. I circled the words *damp* and *warm* in my notes. This was actually just like my bread experiments.

"Gorp, I solved your problem!"

CHAPTER 4

AN EASY FIX?

"Mold grows quickly when things are damp and warm," I explained to Gorp. "When you get back to your cave, your fur must still be a little *damp*. And then you go to sleep in your *warm* cave. It's the perfect way to grow mold."

He looked worried. "You mean, the problem is my warm cave? I don't want to sleep outside in the cold!"

I patted his arm. "I think if we take care of the damp fur, you'll be fine sleeping in your warm cave. You can borrow one of our towels. Use it to get your fur completely dry. And just to be extra safe, take your bath earlier in the day so your fur is *super* dry by the time you get to your warm cave. That should stop the mold from growing."

I wrote in my journal:

SOLUTION:

1. Gorp will take bath early in day.

2. Gorp will use towel to get very dry.

I touched the page I was writing on. I kind of wanted to add a photo of Gorp to my journal entry. My mom had given me an instant film camera, and I was allowed to take one photo of each magical creature I helped. But I was nervous to ask him since we'd just met. Anyway, his problem had been so *easy* to solve. I closed my science journal.

"I'll be right back," I announced. I ran inside and returned with a towel for Gorp.

He picked it up between two fingers and peered at it.

Oh, right. A monster wouldn't actually

know what a towel was. "Here, you use it like this," I said as I pretended to dry myself.

Gorp watched closely and then smiled and took the towel. "Thank you for your help, small human. I am very excited to be able to go to the Monster Ball."

"No problem. And my name is Zoey, and this is Sassafras. We hope you have fun at the dance."

Well, that was easy! I waved good-bye, and Gorp disappeared into the forest. As I turned back to the house, I heard my mom's car coming up the driveway. Sassafras and I hurried to meet her.

"Mom! I solved a problem all by myself! There was a monster and Sassafras loved him. But the monster was covered in mold. We were super careful not to touch him, since I know some molds are dangerous. Anyway, I figured out his fur

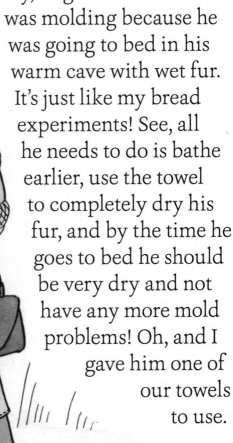

was molding because he was going to bed in his warm cave with wet fur. It's just like my bread experiments! See, all he needs to do is bathe earlier, use the towel to completely dry his fur, and by the time he goes to bed he should be very dry and not have any more mold problems! Oh, and I gave him one of our towels to use.

I hope that's OK."

"Phew! That sounds like quite the afternoon adventure," Mom said. She put her arm around me, and we walked into the house. "I wonder why Sassafras loved him so much?"

"Oh, you should've seen it, Mom. Sassafras was *desperate* to love him. He even tried to jump into Gorp's arms. Gorp was terrified. I don't think monsters see many cats."

Mom nodded thoughtfully. "No, I don't imagine they do. Poor Gorp. Monsters take such pride in being clean. Having moldy fur must be hard on him."

"Yes, he seemed really worried about what the other monsters thought of him. He said he's always stayed home from the Monster Ball because of it."

"Oh, that's a shame! I've heard such wonderful stories about the Monster Ball. It sounds like so much fun. Well, I hope he'll feel brave enough to go this year. It sounds like you did some good work."

I just *knew* I'd solved Gorp's problem, especially after talking to my mom. I was so sure that I flipped my science journal to a new entry and began to daydream about what sort of magical animal we'd meet next.

CHAPTER 5
HE'S BACK

I was in the barn, trying to think of a new experiment to run with the last few pieces of bread, when the doorbell rang. I jumped to my feet so quickly, my Thinking Goggles tumbled off. I grabbed them and ran.

Sassafras practically danced over to the back door.

"What sort of animal do you think it will be this time, Sassafras?"

"Meow?"

"Yeah, I don't know either. Hopefully a baby something, though. Little Marshmallow was the cutest!"

"Meow!"

I opened the door slowly so I wouldn't startle the animal who had come for help. My shoulders slumped. It wasn't a new creature at all. It was Gorp. And he was *still moldy*. Oh no!

Gorp sighed. I frowned. The only happy one was Sassafras. He pranced around purring and *oozing* happiness. He was so happy, in fact, he didn't even notice the fly buzzing around. This was huge because Sassafras is obsessed with chasing and eating bugs. I snatched him up before he had a chance to scare Gorp again.

"It didn't work at all." Gorp kicked at the ground. "I tried everything you said. I bathed early in the day. I used your towel. I made extra sure that my fur was dry before I went to sleep. But I am still moldy!"

He looked like he was about to cry. Then the fly circled around Gorp's head. He tried to swat it away, but it wouldn't leave.

"I'm so gross that this fly won't even leave me alone!" he wailed.

"Gorp, please don't cry! Don't give up yet. The first thing we tried didn't work, but that doesn't mean we can't solve your

problem. We've just got to try something else."

"But *what*?" cried Gorp. "Nothing will fix my moldy fur. I'll be covered in mold forever and ever. I'll never get to go to the dance! *Never!*"

Sassafras wrestled out of my arms and ran up to Gorp. Sassafras' snuggles always make me feel better when I'm crying, but

Gorp saw him coming and backed up.

I managed to grab Sassafras. "Stay!" I instructed.

He gave me a stinky look, but sat down by my feet.

"I know you don't see a lot of cats, but they aren't mean, and they don't eat monsters. You really don't need to be scared of Sassafras. He wouldn't hurt a fly!"

Just as I said it, that pesky fly flew by Sassafras. And he ate it.

Gorp shrieked.

Whoops. I tossed Sassafras in the barn and shut the door. I patted Gorp's arm until he started to breathe more normally. Then it was time to get to work.

"What to try . . . what to try," I muttered as I tapped my Thinking Goggles. "Oh! I should try lots of things. I should run an *experiment*!" I could try adding a bunch of different things to Gorp's fur to stop it from molding.

"Bingo! Give me a minute, Gorp. I need

to grab something from my house."

I held on to my goggles and dashed into the house to grab some ziplock bags and scissors. I wasn't sure what to try on Gorp's fur yet, but I knew I'd need several fur samples to get started.

When I returned to the barn, I didn't see Gorp anywhere. Oh no.

"Gorp? Gorp, are you here? Where did you go?"

The trees rustled, and I heard someone breathing hard. I looked up, and Gorp peered down at me.

"Your cat was scratching at the barn door with his ferocious claws. He was trying to get out so he could eat me while you were gone. It was safer to wait in a tree. Is it OK to come down? Did he break through the door?"

"No, he's still in the barn. I promise I'll protect you if you come down."

Gorp slowly climbed to the ground. "What are those bags for?"

"I'm going to find something we can put on your fur that will stop the mold from growing. To figure out what works best, I'll try a bunch of things and compare them. I'm going to need some fur samples for my experiment. Is that OK?"

Gorp sighed and dropped his shoulders. "I guess that makes sense. Just don't take too much. Or give me a funny haircut."

I nodded. How many things should I try? I wasn't sure. Maybe five samples would be good. I'd need to leave one sample alone. That way I could see how much mold normally grew on Gorp's fur. Then I could add different things to the other samples to try to stop the mold from growing.

I used the length of my pointer finger to measure a piece of orange fur on Gorp's back. I needed some way to make sure I'd have the same amount of hair each time. In an experiment, you change only *one* thing and keep everything else the same. Since I was changing what I was *adding* to the fur, I'd need to keep the *amount* of fur the same.

Gorp wiggled and peered over his shoulder. "You're going to cut hair off of my *back*? Maybe this is a bad idea. Having weird bald patches on my back might be even worse than having mold."

I sighed. "How about I take the samples from down here by your foot? I don't think anyone will notice if you have less hair all the way down at the ground."

"I guess," grumbled Gorp. "If you really mess up, I suppose I can always wear socks to the Monster Ball."

He was finally holding still, so I worked quickly. I was careful not to touch any of the mold. "Ta-da!" I announced. "I've got five fur samples. Bet you can't even tell that I took any hair."

Gorp held his foot out and twisted it left and right. He grunted in approval. "So if I come back later today, you'll have a fix for the mold?"

"Well, no. It'll probably take me at least two days to get results."

"Two days? But you'll definitely have an answer then?"

"Well, I hope so," I said cheerfully.

"You hope so?!" he yelped.

"But the Monster

Ball is in six days! What if you don't figure it out in time?"

"You know, you could always go even if we don't solve this. Sassafras and I love being your friends. We don't mind that you have a little mold on your fur. I'm sure you have some nice monster friends who don't mind either."

Gorp threw his hands in the air. "I can't show up at the dance moldy. It would be *the worst*. I hate being moldy. I hate it!"

Poor Gorp. He was super worried about this moldy fur. We had to figure out a solution!

"Don't worry. I'm going to try a bunch of things in my experiment. I'm sure that one of them will work!"

Gorp sniffled and wiped his nose. He nodded.

After he left, I ran back to the house with my bags of monster fur and washed my hands carefully. I had two days to figure out a solution. The clock was ticking.

CHAPTER 6
PLAYDOUGH

I sat and thought. And then I stood and thought. And then I walked around and thought.

What could I add to stop the mold from growing on Gorp's fur? My investigations with the bread had been about getting *more* mold to grow, not about stopping it from growing at all. The bread in the freezer never grew any mold. But putting Gorp in a freezer was probably not the sort of solution he had in mind.

I sat down at our dining room table. Sassafras jumped into my lap. I petted him and stared at the messy table, covered with my art projects and things I'd invented using stuff my mom saved for me from our recycling.

Maybe my Thinking Goggles weren't positioned right. I moved them to the spot on my head I figured was closest to my

brain and waited. I was looking at all the things on the table when a word started bouncing around in my head. Playdough. *Playdough?*

"OK, Thinking Goggles. If you say so," I muttered. I started playing with the playdough and waited for more inspiration from my goggles.

I made a little Gorp out of playdough.

Sassafras saw the playdough Gorp and purred. I laughed. Boy did my cat *love* Gorp!

I was making a little Sassafras to put next to the little Gorp when it hit me. The moldy playdough! Of course!

One time I'd wanted to make a batch of sparkly grape-scented playdough. I gathered up all of my supplies, but the salt container was almost empty. It only had a teaspoon of salt left in it. The playdough recipe said I needed two-thirds of a cup of salt.

I decided to add the teaspoon of salt and hoped the playdough would still turn out fine.

And it did. Well, at first. I went to grab it a few days later, and it was completely fuzzy with mold. I was shocked. I brought the container to my mom to show her.

"Salt keeps the playdough fresh," she'd said. "If there's not enough salt, the playdough will mold." Mom called the salt a special word. What was it again?

It started with a p ... p ... p ... This was going to drive me nuts!

I heard the front door close. Phew. Mom was here. She could remind me. And I bet she'd also know what to put on Gorp's fur.

CHAPTER 7
KITCHEN SCIENCE

"Mom!" I hollered. "What is that p-word? For salt? In playdough?"

"Well, hello to you too, Zoey!" My mom chuckled as she came into the room. "Salt is a *preservative*. A preservative is an ingredient you add to keep mold and bacteria from growing. That way, whatever you're making will last longer. But why the sudden interest in preservatives?"

"Gorp still needs my help. My towel idea didn't work. I was thinking there must be something about his monster fur that makes mold grow like crazy, even if it's dry."

"Poor Gorp. That mold must really like his fur. Was he terribly disappointed?"

"He was so sad. He even cried! I feel so bad for him. The Monster Ball is only a few days away now. I've *got* to figure this out."

"So, you're thinking of trying something with salt?" Mom asked.

"Yeah. I put on my Thinking Goggles, and I remembered that salt keeps our playdough from growing mold. But I should test some more things in case the salt doesn't work, right? I can test three more things. What else should I try?"

Mom smiled at me. "I bet you can figure that out all by yourself."

"OK. Ummm . . . ?"

"Why don't I give you some clues, and if you can't figure it out by the end of the day, I'll let you know what I would try?"

I smiled. Clues would be a big help.

"What's my first clue?"

"Well, there are lots of different ways to preserve things against mold. Some preservatives are made in big factories, so we obviously can't use those. But lots of preservatives can be found in our kitchen. What do you think you should look at?"

"Hmmm. Preservatives make things last a lot longer. So food that lasts a long time?"

Mom nodded. "You're on the right track, kiddo. See if you can figure out what the preservatives might be by looking at the stickers with the printed ingredient lists."

"To the kitchen, Sassafras!" I announced. "We're going on a preservative hunt!"

CHAPTER 8

THE PRESERVATIVE HUNT

"Preservatives, preservatives. Where are you, preservatives?" I muttered as I walked around the kitchen. I decided to start by looking on our counters. I saw some cooking oil we'd had forever and checked the ingredient list. The only ingredient listed was cooking oil. Hmmm. Maybe that was a preservative? I set it aside to check with my mom.

Next, I picked up a can of beans we'd had for at least a year. Beans, water, and salt. Another vote for salt as a great preservative.

A jar of pickles from our garden caught my eye. We'd made them ourselves at the end of last summer, so those were pretty old too. Oh! And Mom had said that pickling the cucumbers would *preserve* them.

I closed my eyes and tried to remember what we added. Tiny cucumbers! They were so cute. Then we poured something

over them. My nose wrinkled from the memory of the smell. It was vinegar! I really don't like the smell of vinegar. Which is funny because I actually use it a lot. I love playing with baking soda and vinegar. I never get tired of watching them foam and bubble when they mix. I used to make horrible faces while I played until my mom invented an awesome trick. She adds a few drops of peppermint extract to each cup of vinegar she gives me. When

I make my pretend volcanoes erupt,
it smells like candy canes are floating
through the air.

Sassafras interrupted my thoughts
with a meow and pawed at the fridge.

"Great idea! I'll check the fridge next."
I grabbed the vinegar and set it next to the
oil.

I opened the fridge and poked around.
Milk, eggs, butter. All had only one
ingredient, like the cooking oil. But unlike
the oil, we kept them in the fridge. So
maybe they didn't prevent mold on their
own. I was pretty sure the cold from the
fridge was keeping them from spoiling.

Then my hand landed on some
raspberry jelly. Hmmm. That was
interesting. I'd been working on eating
this giant jar of jelly for weeks now, and it
was still good. It was in the fridge, but we
also kept fresh raspberries in the fridge,
and black mold spots still started growing
on them after a few days. Which meant

there just might be something special in the jelly to keep it from molding.

I took it out and read the ingredients: raspberries, water, sugar. Sugar? Hmmm. Maybe. I set the jelly on the counter next to my other guesses.

I looked through the pantry next, but all the crackers and cereal I found only listed strange-sounding ingredients at the end. Those were probably the chemicals made in factories my mom had talked about. I couldn't even read some of the names. They sounded like another language!

I smiled down at Sassafras, who had decided to sit on my right foot. "Any other ideas?"

Sassafras seemed to think for a minute and then left the kitchen. I followed. He ended up hopping into my mom's lap and

purring. I guess that meant he was all out of ideas, too!

Mom looked up and smiled. "Do you have some guesses for me?"

I nodded. "We found a bunch of stuff that uses salt. That's a popular preservative. Our next guesses are oil, vinegar, and maybe sugar?"

Mom grinned. "Great work! Those are all preservatives. I think they'd all be great to test. Are you ready to finish setting up your experiment? Just remember to change only *one* thing and ..."

"I know, I know," I interrupted, "and keep everything else the same. I will, Mom."

CHAPTER 9
THE MOLDY FUR EXPERIMENT

I grabbed my bags of monster fur and my science notebook and went into the kitchen. I started writing down all the bits of my experiment so I wouldn't forget what I'd done. It would probably take a day or two before I could even tell if the mold wasn't growing on some of my test fur. I could definitely forget a lot in two days.

QUESTION:
What will stop the mold from growing on Gorp's fur?

Now I needed to make my guess. Which preservative did I think would work? Most of the stuff in the kitchen used salt. It seemed to work for an awful lot of things. So it would probably work on monster fur too.

HYPOTHESIS:
I think salt will stop the mold from growing on Gorp's fur.

All right. Now to decide how much of each preservative to add. I needed to add the same amount each time. Let's see. Maybe two teaspoons would be enough? That seemed good to me.

PROCEDURE:

1. Put the same amount of Gorp's fur in each ziplock bag.

2. Don't add anything to one bag.
   Add 2 teaspoons of oil to another.
   Add 2 teaspoons of vinegar to another.
   Add 2 teaspoons of salt to another.
   Add 2 teaspoons of sugar to another.

3. Seal the bags.

4. Put the bags in the same place in the barn and check every day to see if mold grows.

Phew. That was a lot of writing. I shook out my hand.

First, I sealed the bag with nothing but fur in it. I labeled it so I could remember that it was the one where I didn't add anything. The *nothing* bag should grow mold like normal. In a few days, I could hold it next to the other bags to see if they were doing a better job of stopping the mold.

I got a new bag and added two teaspoons of vinegar and swished it around until all of the monster fur in the bag was wet. I crinkled up my nose. Blech.

I quickly sealed the bag so I wouldn't have to smell it anymore. I labeled it *vinegar*. I did the same thing for the oil bag.

Things were going just fine until I added sugar to the fourth bag.

"Ergh! This isn't working, Sassafras. The sugar keeps falling to the bottom of the bag. Most of it isn't even touching the fur." Maybe it would be fine? No. It was definitely bugging me that it wasn't coating the fur like the vinegar and oil had.

Whump!

Suddenly a big ball of fluffy fur was next to me on the kitchen counter. I was about to yell "*Sassafras! Off the counter!*" when I realized he was bumping his head against the jelly jar. That was weird. Sassafras liked to eat bugs, not jelly!

I popped him down off the counter. Maybe he was trying to tell me to put the jelly back in the fridge? I picked up the jar and glanced over the ingredients one last time. Oh! Water!

I turned around and picked up the can of beans. It had water too. Right. The beans used salt mixed in water, and the jelly used sugar mixed in water. Of course!

I added two teaspoons of water and two teaspoons of salt to a little bowl, and

two teaspoons of water and two teaspoons of sugar to another little bowl. I stirred them both really well. Then I added two teaspoons of the salt water to the *salt* bag and two teaspoons of the sugar water to the *sugar* bag. This time when I swished the ingredients around, the sugar and salt water coated the monster fur instead of falling to the bottom of the bag. In my science journal, I wrote down the change I'd made to the sugar and salt bags.

I clapped my hands together. Perfect! I was ready to move everything to the barn.

Just then my dad walked into the kitchen. I froze. Mom had told me that Dad couldn't see anything magical. Would these bags look empty to him? He'd probably think this was the weirdest experiment ever.

Dad walked over and ruffled my hair. "Experimenting again, Zoey? What's this one about?" He glanced over my journal notes. "Monster fur? That's a cute idea. Are you running a pretend experiment?"

"Ummm . . ."

He lifted up a bag to the light. "It might make it more fun if you had some actual fur in there. Maybe Sassafras could donate some?"

Sassafras growled. I laughed. The bags *did* look empty to my dad!

"That's a great idea, Dad! Thanks," I chirped.

After my dad left, I leaned down and whispered to Sassafras, "Don't worry, you can keep your fur."

Then I gathered up all of my supplies and headed out to the barn. As I laid everything on the barn desk, I thought of poor Gorp's tears. If the things I was trying didn't stop the mold from growing on his fur, there wouldn't be enough time to run another experiment before the Monster Ball. And if Gorp was still moldy, he'd stay home from the dance. Again. My heart dropped. He *had* to go. This experiment *had* to work!

CHAPTER 10
SUCCESS?

It was hard to wait, but mold needs time to grow. So Sassafras and I did our best to stay busy over the next two days. We went for walks in the forest with my mom. We hunted for bugs. I built cat-sized forest houses for Sassafras using sticks and giant leaves.

Finally we couldn't distract ourselves anymore. I grabbed my science notebook and ran out to the barn to see how the experiment was going.

The first bag I checked was the bag with nothing added. There was definitely mold everywhere. Next, I looked at the *oil* bag. There was some mold, but not as much as in the *nothing* bag. So oil had worked a little bit.

Then I looked at the *salt*, *vinegar*, and *sugar* bags. I squealed so loudly that Sassafras jumped into the air with all his fur puffed out. I dropped my science notebook and grabbed Sassafras and

twirled him around.

"It worked, Sassafras! It worked! Salt and vinegar and sugar *all* worked!"

Right then the barn doorbell rang. Perfect timing! I ran to the door and flung it open. I was so excited, I hugged Gorp before I even said hello.

"It worked! I know what to do!" I cheered.

Gorp's eyes got huge. "It worked?" He was so happy, he didn't even notice Sassafras purring and weaving around his legs.

I grabbed Gorp's arm and pulled him into the barn. "Look! We have *three* choices: salt, sugar, and vinegar." I held up the bags.

A smile lit up Gorp's face. "Which should we choose?"

"Good question! Hmmm. You have an awful lot of fur. Let me run in the house and see what we have the most of."

I was halfway out the door when I heard a scuffling noise behind me. I turned around to see Gorp backing into a corner of the barn with a terrified look on his face. I guess he'd finally noticed the purring Sassafras at his feet. I scooped up my cat and ran into the house.

CHAPTER 11
DECISIONS, DECISIONS

I set Sassafras down on the kitchen floor and opened the pantry. The first thing I saw was the salt container. I checked, and it was almost empty. I scooted a bag of flour to the side and found a brand new giant bag of sugar. Hmmm. That might be the winner.

Finally, I looked down at the very bottom of the pantry and found our stash of vinegar. I shook the bottle. Not much left. I'd been making too many baking soda and vinegar volcanoes!

Sugar was the official winner. I set the big bag down on the kitchen table with a *thunk*.

"What else do I need, Sassafras?"

Sassafras impatiently paced by the back door. He wanted more time with Gorp.

I grabbed a plastic pitcher and a big wooden spoon to mix the sugar water. I added some water to the pitcher and piled everything in my arms. I took little steps so I didn't splash the water everywhere.

Sassafras meowed at me the whole way to the barn. I guess I wasn't moving fast enough for him.

Once we got in, I added a good bit of sugar to the water and stirred with my spoon for a minute or two. Then I looked from the pitcher to Gorp. "Um, we should take this outside. It might get a little messy."

We went outside, and I checked Gorp's fur. "Hey, there isn't any mold right now!"

"Oh, that's only because I just bathed in the stream. Is that OK?"

"That's perfect. The sugar water should stop the mold from growing on your fur, like it did with the fur sample in the bag. I'm going to, uh, I guess pour it on a little at a time and spread it around with my spoon. Does that sound OK?"

Gorp nodded and stood very still. Sassafras saw me raise the pitcher up and scooted out of the way. He hates getting wet.

I poured and spread the liquid as best

I could. After a few minutes, I was pretty sure I'd given Gorp's fur a good coating of sugar water.

"Ta-da! You're good to go. If you want to come back in a day or two, I can mix up more for you."

"I can't believe I'm going to the Monster Ball!" Gorp cheered. "I'm a bit damp, so I think I'll take a nice long walk to make sure I'm dry before I settle down for the night."

"That's a great plan, Gorp! I'm so happy for you!"

We waved good-bye to each other, and I brought all of my supplies into the house. After I put everything we'd used in the sink to wash later, I grabbed my science journal and wrote down the results of my monster fur experiment.

I was so happy I'd solved Gorp's mold problem, but as I closed my science journal, I realized I'd forgotten to get a photo of him *again*.

Maybe he'd come back for more sugar water in a few days, and I could ask him then?

CHAPTER 12
OH NO!

Sassafras and I were in the kitchen figuring out what we wanted for breakfast when the magic doorbell rang.

The doorbell this early? I really, really, *really* hoped it wasn't Gorp coming back with mold again.

Mom looked over at me with a raised eyebrow and handed me a piece of toast.

"Thanks, Mom," I said. I grabbed the toast and gave her a quick hug on my way out the door. Sassafras grabbed one big mouthful of cat food, and trotted out the door behind me with stuffed cheeks.

We flew through the barn and threw open the back door. And there was Gorp.

"Gorp! What happened? Why are you all wet?"

Gorp flung his hands in the air.

"Everything went wrong. Everything!" he spluttered. "First, on the walk back to my cave, *everything* stuck to me. Dirt, leaves, twigs, even little flying bugs! I looked ridiculous."

Ohhh no. Of course sugar water would be sticky! Why hadn't I thought of that? I guess because I'd used the spoon instead of my hands, I didn't feel the stickiness at all.

He continued, "I thought that was the worst of it, but I was wrong. It got much worse. I woke up to ants crawling all over me this morning. Even in my *ears*."

Ohhh no. I'd forgotten how much ants like sweet things. And sugar water is very sweet. Gorp must have seemed like a giant monster-shaped candy to the ants!

"I ran and jumped into the stream and then came straight here," he said. "My fur didn't get any mold, but this was So! Much! Worse!"

"Oh, Gorp! I'm so so sorry. I can't believe I didn't think of the stickiness or the ants."

Oh man, I had totally messed up. I put my head in my hands. I was too embarrassed to look Gorp in the eye.

Sassafras bumped my leg. "Mrrrw?"

I looked down to see why he was making that weird noise, and he had a ziplock bag in his mouth. Of course!

"Sassafras! You're a genius!" I picked

him up and kissed him on the head. Gorp made a sour face. "It's not over yet. We still have two more things we can try. And this time, I promise I'll choose more carefully."

I opened the bag marked *salt* that Sassafras had brought over. I reached in to feel. My shoulders slumped. "No! The salt water fur is sticky, too."

Gorp's eyes filled with tears and his lip

trembled. "I give up! Nothing will work. I'll never get to go to the Monster Ball."

"Don't cry, Gorp! We still have the vinegar to try," I said. But I was worried.

I took a deep breath. This had to work. Vinegar wasn't sticky, right? My hands were never sticky after playing with baking soda and vinegar. A little gritty from the baking soda, maybe. But no, definitely not sticky.

I slowly reached one finger inside the bag. I gave the vinegar-covered Gorp fur a quick poke. I looked up at Gorp and smiled.

"Feel it!" I took his hand and put it inside the bag.

"It's not sticky!" A smile slowly spread over Gorp's face.

He grabbed a handful of the vinegar fur from inside the bag and pulled it out. Then he twisted his head to the side, squeezed his eyes closed, and stuck out his tongue.

"This smells terrible! Oh no! I can't *stink*," he wailed.

The vinegar smell made me wrinkle my nose, too. It did stink. In fact, I *hated* the smell of vinegar . . . which is why I had a solution.

I grabbed Gorp by the shoulders. "It's going to be OK. Trust me. I can fix the smell. Wait here."

I ran into the house and quickly searched the pantry until I found a tiny bottle of peppermint extract.

"Thanks, Mom!" I whispered as I grabbed it and the bottle of vinegar and dashed to the barn.

Gorp had stopped crying, but I could tell that after all these ups and downs, he didn't think he'd ever go to the Monster Ball.

I twisted the cap off the vinegar bottle and added a few drops of peppermint

extract into it. I put the cap back on and shook the vinegar bottle twice.

I poured some of the new vinegar over Gorp's fur sample. "Smell it now."

Gorp took a small sniff. Then a bigger sniff. Then a really, really big sniff.

"That smells *wonderful*," he exclaimed. "And it won't make me sticky? Ants don't like vinegar, right?"

"No, it's not sticky. And ants don't like it. You can go to the Monster Ball and you won't be moldy and you'll smell like *candy canes*!"

Gorp grabbed me in a giant, wet, furry monster hug, and I couldn't stop smiling. I was so relieved to find something that worked.

Gorp held the bottle to his chest and gave me a huge smile. "Thank you, Zoey. This means so much to me."

I was super excited for Gorp. I kind of wished that *I* could go to the Monster Ball too, and see him at the ball with all his friends.

Then it hit me. The camera! Maybe Gorp could take a picture for me while he was there. It wouldn't be as good as going myself, but when you take a photo of a magical creature, some of the magic *stays* in the photo. So, having the photo would be like having a little bit of the Monster Ball with me.

"Uh, Gorp? Before you go – can I ask you a favor? Would you be willing to borrow my camera and take a picture at the Monster Ball? Then maybe afterward you could come by for a visit and tell me all about it?"

Before he had a chance to say no, I ran into the barn and grabbed my science journal and my camera. I showed him how the camera worked and what a photo was.

He carefully picked up the camera with one hand and looked at it. "I will bring your machine to the dance with me and I will do my best to get you a photo."

CHAPTER 13

THANK YOU

Sassafras watched from the edge of my sandbox as I erupted one of my sand volcanoes. After hearing about our success, Mom had taken a special trip to the store to stock up on vinegar.

I buried another plastic bottle with baking soda inside under the sand. I made sure that only the opening of the bottle peeked out, and then I reached for more peppermint-scented vinegar.

The smell of the peppermint reminded

me of Gorp. Today was Friday, and Gorp had told us that the Monster Ball was on Thursday. I was hoping that he'd gone and had a great time.

I poured the vinegar into the bottle. Some of the white bubbles flowed down the side of the volcano and got on

Sassafras' paw. He leapt up and shook his paw wildly to get the bubbles off.

"Oh, Sassafras!" I couldn't help laughing.

Suddenly he froze mid-paw shake and took off purring into the forest.

I stood up. Could it be Gorp?

I ran after Sassafras and found him at Gorp's feet. He was, once again, staring up lovingly at the big monster.

Gorp looked worried until he saw me. Then he smiled. He had my camera and a photo in one hand, but the other hand was hidden behind his back.

I couldn't wait to see the photo of the Monster Ball! I ran over to him and gave him a big hug.

"Zoey! Thank you for all of your work solving my mold problem. I had a great time at the Monster Ball. See?"

Gorp handed me the photo. He looked fancy in a bow tie and had his arms around two other monsters. All three were

laughing. In fact . . . I thought I could hear it. I put my ear closer and grinned. The sound of deep belly laughs was definitely coming from the photo.

"I can see and *hear* that you had a great time!" I held it up to Gorp's ear.

"Whoooa," he said.

I pointed to a cake in the background. "And there was cake?"

"Yes! My aunt's famous mud cake with

grub sprinkles. Delicious."

My stomach flipped at the thought of *grub* sprinkles. "Oh, uh, yum," I managed to squeak out.

"I should have saved you a slice!" He shook his head. "I did get you these, though." Clutched in the hand he'd been hiding behind his back was a big bunch of green and brown weeds, complete with dirt-covered roots.

I stared for a minute, not sure what to make of it.

Gorp pushed it toward me one more time. "It's a *bouquet.* For you, Zoey!"

Ohhh! I took the "bouquet" of weeds and grinned. "Thank you so much, Gorp! You didn't have to get me anything, though. I'm so glad you finally went to the Monster Ball!"

"Me too. Do you know what the funniest part was? Everyone kept asking where I'd been at the other monster parties. And when I talked about my

moldy fur, they all said they didn't care about it. I was worried about nothing this whole time. Although I must admit, I enjoy no longer being moldy. And now I smell *so* good!"

I sniffed the air and caught a whiff of candy cane. *Yum.* "You sure do!"

He glanced over his shoulder. "I'm sorry I can't stay for long. I promised my friends I'd go hunt for glowing salamanders with them."

"I hope you'll still come visit us sometimes. We'd be happy to make sure you always have peppermint-y vinegar for your fur."

Gorp gave me one last hug, and then he reached a finger down and gently tapped Sassafras once on the head. Sassafras dissolved into loud, rumbly purring. Gorp smiled uneasily and waved. Then he headed into the forest to play with his monster friends.

Sassafras and I went into the house. I grabbed a vase, filled it with water, and tried to arrange the weeds. As well as anyone could arrange a bouquet of weeds, anyway.

My dad came into the kitchen and raised an eyebrow when he saw what I was doing.

"It's a bouquet from a friend," I told him.

"Kind of a strange friend you've got there, Zoey. Aren't bouquets supposed to be made of flowers?"

I laughed and nodded.

I took the bouquet into my room and set it on my desk next to my science journal. Sassafras jumped up and pawed at the pages of the journal until it opened to Gorp's picture. He rubbed his face against it, purring super loudly. Then he drooled a little on Gorp's photo.

"Ewww, Sassafras! That's so gross!" I flipped to a new blank page in the science journal to keep the photo safe from further cat drool.

As I left my room with Sassafras tucked under my arm, I turned back to look at my open journal on the desk. I couldn't help but grin, imagining what magical friend we'd meet next.

GLOSSARY

Conclusion: What you learned from your experiment (hopefully you get an answer to your question but sometimes you don't)

Experiment: What you do to answer your question

Hypothesis: What you think will happen in your experiment

Materials: All the things you need to do your experiment

Mold: A kind of fluffy looking fungus that breaks down (eats) dead things

Preservative: Something that keeps mold from growing

Procedure: What you do in your experiment (the steps)

Solution: An answer to the problem

ABOUT THE AUTHOR AND ILLUSTRATOR

ASIA CITRO used to be a science teacher, but now she plays at home with her two kids and writes books. When she was little, she had a cat just like Sassafras. He loved to eat bugs and always made her laugh (his favorite toy was a plastic human nose that he carried everywhere). Asia has also written three activity books: *150+ Screen-Free Activities for Kids, The Curious Kid's Science Book,* and *A Little Bit of Dirt.* She has yet to find a baby dragon in her backyard, but she always keeps an eye out, just in case.

MARION LINDSAY is a children's book illustrator who loves stories and knows a good one when she reads it. She likes to draw anything and everything but does spend a completely unfair amount of time drawing cats. Sometimes she has to draw dogs just to make up for it. She illustrates picture books and chapter books as well as painting paintings and designing patterns. Like Asia, Marion is always on the lookout for dragons and sometimes thinks there might be a small one living in the airing cupboard.

for activities and more visit
ZOEYANDSASSAFRAS.COM

31901061008217